I Have a New Baby Brother

I have a new baby brother.

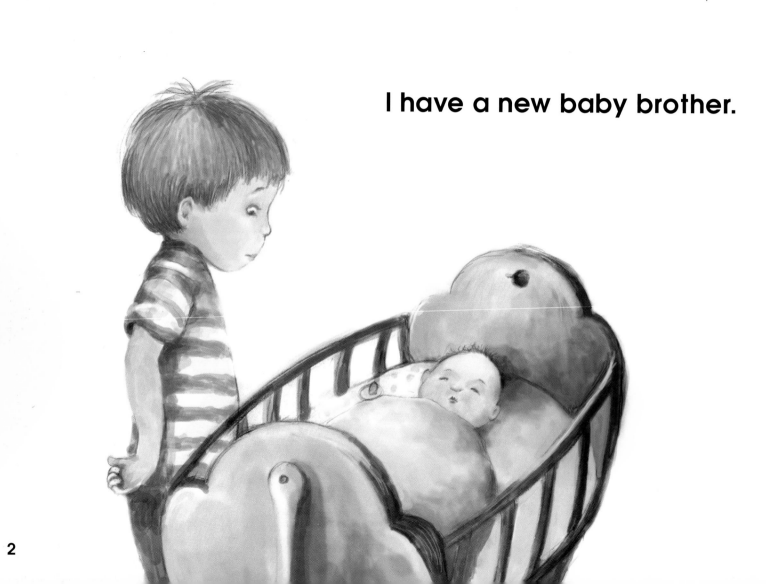

I wanted a puppy or a kitten.
But I got a baby brother.

3

If we had bears, I could have a bear cub.

If we had tigers, I could have a tiger cub.
But I got a baby brother.

If we had elephants,
I could have an elephant calf.

If we had walruses, I could have a walrus calf.
But I got a baby brother.

If we had wolves, I could have a wolf pup.

If we had seals, I could have a seal pup.
But I got a baby brother.

9

If we had sheep,
I could have a lamb.

If we had pigs,
I could have a piglet.
But I got a baby brother.

If we had ducks, I could have a duckling.

If we had zebras, I could have a colt.
But I got a baby brother.

If we had kangaroos, I could have a joey.

But I got a new baby brother named

Joey!

16